"ME COOKIE!"

By Emma Jones

Illustrated by Maggie Swanson

Featuring Jim Henson's Sesame Street Muppets

A GOLDEN BOOK • NEW YORK

Published by Golden Books Publishing Company, Inc.,
in conjunction with Children's Television Workshop

One spring morning a little blue monster was born.
He was soft and furry and not much bigger than a loaf
of bread.

The sweet smell from a bakery drifted through an
open window in the nursery. "That smells like cookies
baking," said one of the nurses.

The little newborn smiled. "Coo," he said.

"What a clever little monster," said the nurse. "I
think he's trying to say 'cookie.'"

That clever little monster was a happy baby. He smiled and gurgled and liked to play with his toes.

He was also a good eater and always drank his
bottle down to the last drop.

Baby Monster's favorite sound was "coo," and he said it nearly all the time. Someone thought he was trying to say "cool." Someone else thought he was trying to say "coop."

He tried again and again, until one day he said a whole word. "Coo—coo—cookie!" he cried.

From that day on, "cookie" was Baby Monster's favorite word, and cookies, of course, were his favorite food.

"Me cookie" was the first thing he said when he woke up in the morning.

"Me cookie" was the last thing he said when he was tucked into his crib at night.

The little monster grew quickly. No one had to tell him to clean his plate, although sometimes he had to be reminded not to eat the plate.

"No, no, Baby Monster," said his baby-sitter.

"Me cookie," he answered.

"No cookies now," said the baby-sitter. "It's time for your bath."

Baby Monster liked bathtime. He soon learned that soap did not taste at all like cookies.

It wasn't long before Baby Monster learned to walk. He took his very first step toward the cookie jar.

By now that little monster had discovered all kinds of ways of getting cookies. Sometimes, just by looking hungry, he could get someone to give him a cookie.

Sometimes he could get a cookie when no one was looking. If all else failed, Baby Monster cried, "COOKIE!" as loud as he could.

Baby Monster liked many other kinds of food besides cookies. One time he pulled up all the carrots in the neighbor's garden and ate every one of them.

"No, no, Baby Monster," cried the neighbor when she saw what he had done.

"Me cookie," said the little monster.

"Oh, all right," answered the neighbor. She went inside to get him a cookie.

It wasn't long before Baby Monster could say all
kinds of words. "Cake!" the little monster would shout.
"Apple. Ice cream. Broccoli. Pizza!"

Baby Monster liked nursery rhymes. His favorite was "Peter, Peter, Pumpkin Eater." He liked "Little Miss Muffet," too—and wondered what curds and whey tasted like.

At Baby Monster's birthday party, he ate his birthday cake—all by himself.

At Ernie's birthday party, he ate Ernie's birthday cake—all by himself.

It soon became clear that if Baby Monster was at a birthday party, there had to be two cakes—one for Baby Monster and one for everyone else.

Baby Monster grew to be a big little monster.
His favorite toy was his play kitchen.
His favorite place in the park was the sandbox,
where he made sand-cakes and sand-pies and
sand-wiches.

lyear
9
months

6
months

He was a happy little monster except for one thing, and that thing was his name. Every time someone called him Baby, he would say, "Me cookie."

Sometimes he would get a cookie and sometimes he wouldn't, but each time he would think, "Oh, brother, why they not understand?"

One day that blue monster decided to do something drastic. When his baby-sitter called him Baby, he said, "Me cookie," just like he always did. But this time, when he was handed a cookie, he shook his head and said, "No."

"No?" cried his baby-sitter. "Are you feeling all right?"

"Me feel fine, but me not Baby Monster, me Cookie Monster!"

"Oh, I get it. Cookie Monster is your name!" said the baby-sitter.

"At last someone get it," said the happy Cookie Monster, and he grabbed the cookie and gobbled it down.

And to this day, no one has ever called that furry blue monster anything but Cookie Monster.